In 1935 if you wanted to
read a good book, you needed
either a lot of money or a library card.
Cheap paperbacks were available, but their
poor production generally mirrored the quality
between the covers. One weekend that year,
Allen Lane, Managing Director of The Bodley Head,
having spent the weekend visiting Agatha Christie,
found himself on a platform at Exeter station trying to
find something to read for his journey back to London.
He was appalled by the quality of the material he had to
choose from. Everything that Allen Lane achieved from that
day until his death in 1970 was based on a passionate belief
in the existence of 'a vast reading public for intelligent
books at a low price'. The result of his momentous vision
was the birth not only of Penguin, but of the 'paperback
revolution'. Quality writing became available for the price of
a packet of cigarettes, literature became a mass medium
for the first time, a nation of book-borrowers became a
nation of book-buyers – and the very concept of book
publishing was changed for ever. Those founding
principles – of quality and value, with an overarching
belief in the fundamental importance of reading –
have guided everything the company has
done since 1935. Sir Allen Lane's
pioneering spirit is still very much alive
at Penguin in 2005. Here's to
the next 70 years!

MORE THAN A BUSINESS

'We decided it was time to end the almost customary half-hearted manner in which cheap editions were produced – as though the only people who could possibly want cheap editions must belong to a lower order of intelligence. We, however, believed in the existence in this country of a vast reading public for intelligent books at a low price, and staked everything on it'
Sir Allen Lane, 1902–1970

'The Penguin Books are splendid value for sixpence, so splendid that if other publishers had any sense they would combine against them and suppress them'
George Orwell

'More than a business ... a national cultural asset'
Guardian

'When you look at the whole Penguin achievement you know that it constitutes, in action, one of the more democratic successes of our recent social history'
Richard Hoggart

Short Short Stories

DAVE EGGERS

PENGUIN BOOKS

PENGUIN BOOKS

Published by the Penguin Group
Penguin Books Ltd, 80 Strand, London WC2R ORL, England
Penguin Group (USA) Inc., 375 Hudson Street, New York, New York 10014, USA
Penguin Group (Canada), 10 Alcorn Avenue, Toronto, Ontario, Canada M4V 3B2
(a division of Pearson Penguin Canada Inc.)
Penguin Ireland, 25 St Stephen's Green, Dublin 2, Ireland
(a division of Penguin Books Ltd)
Penguin Group (Australia), 250 Camberwell Road, Camberwell, Victoria 3124,
Australia (a division of Pearson Australia Group Pty Ltd)
Penguin Books India Pvt Ltd, 11 Community Centre,
Panchsheel Park, New Delhi – 110 017, India
Penguin Group (NZ), cnr Airborne and Rosedale Roads, Albany,
Auckland 1310, New Zealand (a division of Pearson New Zealand Ltd)
Penguin Books (South Africa) (Pty) Ltd, 24 Sturdee Avenue,
Rosebank 2196, South Africa

Penguin Books Ltd, Registered Offices: 80 Strand, London WC2R ORL, England

www.penguin.com

These stories first appeared in the *Guardian* in 2004
Published as a Pocket Penguin 2005

1

Set in 11/13pt Monotype Dante
Typeset by Palimpsest Book Production Limited
Polmont, Stirlingshire
Printed in England by Clays Ltd, St Ives plc

Contents

You Know How to Spell Elijah

You are at the airport, airless, and sitting in a black faux-leather chair near your departure gate. There is a girl, about twelve, sitting in a similar chair, across the wide immaculate aisle, and she wants to know how to spell Elijah. She is working on a crossword in *Teen* magazine, and is squinting at it, chewing her inner mouth. She is flanked by her parents, and soon appeals to them for help. Her father is burly and bearded, her mother tall and thin. Her mother, who reminds you of a praying mantis, answers her daughter's question this way: 'It's easy, Dakota: E-L-I-S-H-A.' And though you have your own things to do, your own *Boating Week* to read and your bagel to eat, you can no longer concentrate on anything but this young girl's crossword puzzle, quickly being polluted by the advice of these people she calls her parents. (And the young girl is working not in pencil – fool! – but in pen.) You are burning to tell her the truth about the young actor's name-spelling, but fear you would embarrass or undermine her mother, which you don't want to do. Besides, you think, the girl's father will surely correct the mother; isn't that the beauty of the two-parent system? Indeed it is, for here he is now, leaning over, inspecting the crossword like a good dad. And now he is putting on his glasses even, and finally he tells her, 'No, Dakota. I'm pretty sure it's A-L-I-G-A.' Fucking christ! You let out a quick desperate cough. These people, you think, cannot be serious. This poor girl, stuck forever in a dim, ill-spelling world, nowhere to turn. She'll never know the spelling of Elijah, or Enrique, or even Justin or J. C. Should you intervene? Isn't it your duty? Don't those who know the truth have a responsibility to stop the dissemination of untruths? Standing idly by is tantamount to complicity, a partnership in ignorance! You must step in. You can do so good-naturedly. You can do so without upsetting the family unit, the sanctity thereof. But you're eighteen feet away, making it impossible without implying that you were paying much too much attention to the girl's crossword than would seem casual or proper. They'll assume you have an unhealthy interest in *Teen* magazine and its cover boys. And really now, what *were* you doing, listening in to her spelling request? Why *had* you directed your attention her way? What's wrong with you, anyway? Isn't your own life complicated enough? Is your own existence so free of mistakes that you need to seek them out in strangers at airports, inserting yourself into the life of a twelve-year-old with a crush on a hobbit-playing actor? No wonder you're on your way to a spa in Palm Desert. You damn well need the rest.

This Certain Song

There is a couple named Francis and Therese; they both
have wide feet and believe they are in love. They have
been together a year and have once, while tipsy,
mumbled reciprocal I love yous. At issue: Yesterday
Francis bought an album by a band named Wheat, and
on it there is a song called 'I Met a Girl', the lyrics of
which include: 'I met a girl I'd like to know better/ But
I'm already with someone.' It's a very catchy song, and
Francis is sure that its appeal to him is confined to its
tune, its melody – whatever you call how a song is put
together and how it sounds. But because Francis has
played the song many times in the house, and in the
car, and hums the song constantly, Therese, who prefers
Brecht and Weill, is convinced that there is more to his
obsession than the tuneness of this tune. Have you met
someone you'd like to know better? she asks. He laughs.
She laughs too, without mirth, and she asks it again,
now holding a bread knife, semi-casually. He laughs
again, then stops laughing, and thinks. Could it be that
this song articulates something that he's felt secretly,
ever since he went to work for the hemp-based toy store?
At work there are six perfectly charming women his
age – Gwen, Gina, Gia, Georgia, Gretchen and Gop –
all attractive, all single. He calls them the G-6, and is
proud of having invented this nickname, but he has not

socialized with them outside of work, not even for lunch. So *is* there anything else to him and the G-6? He finally decides that there is not. He does love Therese, and wants to assuage her fears. He knows all too well the trouble such a song – the right tune, the wrong words – can have on a relationship. It was not long ago he was dating someone else, Charisse, while enamored of the band called Prodigy. Did she understand his love of the song 'Smack My Bitch Up'? Somehow, she did not.

What the Water Feels Like to the Fishes

Like the fur of a chinchilla. Like the cleanest tooth.
Yes, the fishes say, this is what it feels like. People always
ask the fishes, 'What does the water feel like to you?'
and the fishes are always happy to oblige. Like feathers are to other feathers, they say. Like powder touch-
ing ash. When the fishes tell us these things, we begin
to understand. We begin to think we know what the
water feels like to the fishes. But it's not always like fur
and ash and the cleanest tooth. At night, they say, the
water can be different. At night, when it's very cold, it
can be like the tongue of a cat. At night, when it's very
very cold, the water is like cracked glass. Or honey. Or
forgiveness, they say, ha ha. When the fishes answer
these questions – which they are happy to do – they
also ask why. They are curious, fish are, and thus they
ask Why? Why do you want to know what the water
feels like to the fishes? And we are never quite sure. The
fishes press further. Do you breathe air? they ask. The
answer, we say, is yes. Well then, they say, What does
the air feel like to you? And we do not know. We think
of air and we think of wind, but that's another thing.
Wind is air in action, air on the move, and the fishes
know this. Well then, they ask again, what does the air
feel like? And we have to think about this. Air feels like
air, we say, and the fishes laugh mirthlessly. Think! they

say. Think, they say, now gentler. And we think and we guess that it feels like hair, thousands of hairs, swaying ever so slightly in breezes microscopic. The fishes laugh again. Do better, think harder, they say. It feels like language, we say, and they are impressed. Keep going, they say. It feels like blood, we say, and they say No, no, that's not it. The air is like being wanted, we say, and they nod approvingly. The air is like getting older, they say, and they smile their big fish smiles.

The Weird Wife

He was married to a weird wife. He knew this one day when they were at the water. They had been swimming earlier, in very watery green water, and as they sat on the rocks, white and warm, he asked her, 'Do I want to swim again?' He did not count on her knowing the answer to this question but she thought about it for a moment and said, 'I think you want to swim again.' So he swam again, because it seemed that she was right, and he did enjoy the swimming greatly. He swam straight out into the lake as fast as he could, not taking a breath, and then came back in slowly, doing the breast-stroke and watching her standing on the rocks, trying to chase away a bee with her towel. After he dried off they walked up the rocky path, and he thought about how weird it was that she had known he had wanted to swim again. Later, they sat on the porch of the house they'd rented, on a hill of crumbling homes, and they hoped that the grasshoppers wouldn't come. Every night they had been coming, huge grasshoppers who leapt into her hair and into his shorts, and they made the porch less pleasant. As they waited and hoped that the grasshoppers had moved on or simultaneously died of a virus, he looked over to her and noticed her nose, which turned upward more than he'd remembered. It was weird how it sort of came to a point and turned upward, wasn't it? She really had a weirdly wonderful nose, but he wasn't sure if he'd ever appreciated it before. He was about to ask her about it when he noticed her shirt, which was orange with creamy white lettering on it, something in Spanish. It was a great shirt on her but he hadn't seen this shirt, he didn't think. He thought it was weird how every few weeks she wore something he hadn't seen before or didn't remember. He would look at her clothes and say, 'I don't remember that shirt' or 'Is that new?' and sometimes the article in question was new and sometimes it wasn't new. But he didn't ask about her nose or her clothes, this night with warm wind coming over this lake in Minnesota, because she would know the answer right away, because she knew so many things – like just when and how softly to touch the area behind his ears while he was driving – and so he'd be left dumb, bewildered, which is the way one often feels in the presence of a someone like this, a wife who is weird.

This Flight Attendant
(Gary, Is It?) Is On Fire!

Have you heard this guy, the flight attendant? You've been asleep, but he's on fire! Listen to this guy! Yeah, the guy making his way down the aisle with the snacks for the passengers – I think his name is Gary. Did you hear what he just said to the pair of young women in Row 14? He said, 'Hey you guys, do you want some cookies?' And when they said 'Sure,' he said 'You do? You want some cookies? You want me to toss my cookies?' And then he threw them the packages of cookies. Holy shit it was funny. You didn't hear that? It was awesome. The girls loved it. I loved it. You don't get it, do you? See, he was actually *throwing* the cookies to them, but when he warned them, he said he was going to '*toss* his *cookies*', which is a euphemism for vomiting. Vomiting's funny, man! C'mon, dude. And it's doubly funny when you're on a *plane*, because sometimes people vomit on planes. Oh man, that one went way over your head. Whatever. Oh wait. Hear that? He just did a perfect Cookie Monster imitation. Hear it? It was flawless. Wow. He really has *presence*, you know? There's something a man like that has, something intangible – you can't learn a gift like that. You're born with it, and you just have to hone it, I guess. He's the same one who did the intro earlier. Remember? He got on the intercom and interspersed jokes between the directions about flotation devices and seatbelts? Remember when he said 'In case of a water landing, your suede boots are toast'? I thought I was gonna spit out my tomato juice. He did it in kind of a gay voice, which is always really funny, to be making the voice of a gay person, like how they all talk. And to be thinking about suede boots at a time like that would be so *absurd*. That's why it's funny, you know? Because it's so crazy to be thinking about boots if you were *crash-landing in an ocean*. I wonder what he'll say next. A guy like that, his mind must run at a different speed than the rest of ours. Like some kind of supercomputer of humor. I'm so glad that this airline encourages its flight attendants to be crazy characters, you know? To personalize their announcements and to joke around. It livens things up, makes your day brighter, makes the flight more memorable. One time on this same airline I had a flight attendant who made such a good joke. Once we had taken off, she said, 'We're now on our way to Nova Scotia, enjoy the flight.' And the funny part was that the flight was actually going to *Miami*, which isn't *anywhere near* Nova Scotia. Everyone on the plane sort of freaked out for a second, and then, when she let us off the hook, everyone laughed and sighed with relief. We didn't want to be going to Greenland, or wherever that is! It's cold *there*, and we were headed somewhere *warm*! We all had a big laugh about that one; for the next four hours of the flight, I kept finding myself chuckling, thinking of the great joke she played on us. But she wasn't as good as this fella. This guy's got something special. Oop – there he goes again. You hear that? He said, 'I'm sorry everyone, but your flight attendant buttons don't work tonight. If you need something, please tell me once we land and I'll do my best to help you.' That's so perfect, because obviously he can't help people with, say, a pillow, once we've already landed! So he's jerking our chain again! Like, avoiding working on the flight! Man, I hope he never stops, because every time he interrupts the music or the movie or wakes me up when I'm trying to sleep – every time that overloud intercom busts through my fuzzy fragile consciousness, I think, 'Oh wow, I can't wait to hear what he says! I cannot mother-fucking wait for one goddamn more second to hear what Gary has to say!'

True Story – 1986 – Midwest – USA – Tuesday

The boy-man is sixteen years old and the gym teacher is distributing towels. The boy-man is sixteen years old and in swimming class and the gym teacher, squinting, is distributing towels. The boy-man is sixteen, in swimming class and the class has been given swimsuits to wear in the pool – they must all wear standard-issue swimsuits, tight, threadbare and bruise-blue. The boy-man is sixteen years old and the gym teacher is distributing towels after class while the boy-man, all the boys, are naked among the cold tile. The boy-man is sixteen years old and cold, naked among the tile, surrounded by other boy-men, each washing the chlorine out of his hair while knowing. The boy-man is sixteen years old, cold, among the other boy-men, and the gym teacher is standing at the end of the row of showers, distributing towels, and the boys are not sure they know. The boy-man is sixteen years old, knows and is cold, while all the boys have peeled off their bruise-blue suits and have deposited them, threadbare but heavy, in the sagging bone-white bin. The boy-man has sixteen years, is cold, but has not reached puberty, and is naked among the other boys and tile, and the gym teacher is standing at the end of the showers, waiting to distribute towels, orange, one per boy. The boy-man is sixteen, old, is late for so many things, and the boys must walk seven steps across the cold tile to reach the gym teacher, who is stout and silver-haired and who watches as they approach, one by one, for their towels, orange. The boy-man is sixteen years old and the gym teacher is distributing towels to the cold naked boys as they walk toward him, as he watches, as he squints and answers the boy-man who knows. When the boy-man, sixteen, asks why the silver-haired gym teacher must stand in the showers, watching, handing the towels to the boys personally as they walk toward him, he says, eyes disappearing in the steam, that otherwise the boys might take not one towel but two, and not one but two will just not do.

It Is Finally Time to Tell the Story

Yes, it is finally time to tell the story about the sheep from that one island whose name is forgotten but which rhymes with Godiva. There were too many sheep on this particular island, so some of them got on a boat and left for Spain. In Spain, however, they were not welcomed. Everyone in Spain, waiting by the shore for the boat to come in, had expected something more unusual than sheep. When the gangway was lowered and the sheep descended, the Spaniards said many things to them, the overall gist of which was 'Go back to your island, sheep, and send some gila monsters or Komodo dragons.' It is well known that the Spanish have always longed for gila monsters and Komodo dragons and perhaps some of those child-sized ancestors of *Homo erectus* everyone's talking about. So the sheep set sail again, this time looking for Franz Josef Land, which they'd heard had a balmy climate and universal health insurance. But when they arrived, six months later, they found neither. Franz Josef Land was desolate, treeless, and obsessed only with wireless internet access. So the sheep set sail again, this time landing in Montana, which no one – no one but these seafaring sheep – realized had a deep-sea port. They walked around Montana for a while, but found the people to be unfriendly and with very poor taste in music. Everywhere they went, they heard Thin Lizzy and Bachman Turner Overdrive, and though the sheep enjoyed much of the music by these bands, they actually preferred early King Crimson and later XTC. So they set sail again, this time looking for – you know what? Hold on a second. Wait one damned second here. The author of this irrelevant narrative just woke up, momentarily, from a self-induced mental coma, and now something is worming into his consciousness. It couldn't be. Did that really happen? Did we really elect Bush again? Holy fucking shit. Screw the sheep and pity us Americans. Have we ever wanted pity before? We have not, but now we do. Shower us with pity as we cloak ourselves in shame.

A Circle Like Some Circles

The fire, behind them in its stone fireplace, is gas-powered but meant to look real, with faux logs and even cinders glowing arythmically. His name is Ron and he is looking at Mina, his friend, who years ago had an accident – a train jumped and other passengers died – and she has been recovering since. Ron is visiting Mina, sitting with her and her grandmother because he visits Mina once a year; it would be more often, but she lives six hours away from Ron and he is lazy. He is looking at Mina, smiling at her; in many ways she seems precisely the same as when she was when they were young together, years before, when they flirted and drove over hills too fast. He is sitting with her and her grandmother, and her grandmother is talking about how she just had the battery on her pacemaker replaced. While she is talking about this, she taps her sternum, bare under her housedress, and Ron shudders. Ron shudders at certain things: certain deformities, makeup on men, people with horrible burns on their face, and the thought of elderly people having their bodies opened up with knives in hospitals. Ron shudders and then stops shuddering and while Mina talks, he looks at her. They are sitting in front of the fire, and her grandmother has ceased talking about the pacemaker, and he is looking at Mina, who he once thought he could marry.

She looks very much the same, huge eyes, even though her brain doesn't work quite the way it did before the accident; thus she lives at home. Mina is talking animatedly, about a new song she's heard, something involving children and destiny, and Ron is looking at her neck, which has a scar that seems new. He is almost sure that this is not a scar from the train accident – those scars are on her back and legs, and he has seen most of those. So where did this one come from? Mina's grandmother, when Ron was planning his visit with her on the phone, had hinted that Mina had had a hard few months; Ron assumes this involved a fall of some kind. He shudders again. He sits near the fire, very warm and shuddering, close to Mina's scar and her grandmother's pacemaker, and he thinks the inevitable thoughts: that there is no God, that there had better not be any kind of God, because he doesn't want someone to blame for all this bullshit.

On Making Someone a Good Man
By Calling Him a Good Man

Stuart has the face of a Scottish warrior. He has been told this, though he is unsure if this means he has a historically accurate and fierce Highlands look, or that he simply looks like a particular actor from *Braveheart*. Stuart has been friends with Margaret since they were very small. Margaret, soft in every way, recently married Phillipe, who is an idiot. Stuart feels no jealously toward Phillipe, for he and Margaret were never romantic, and he actually wanted to like Phillipe, from the start he tried to like Phillipe, but Phillipe has always made this difficult because Phillipe is a moron. Phillipe does not work, or does not work often, and feels no guilt at all about allowing Margaret to pay for food, for car repairs that he makes necessary, and for rent. When he has his own money, he goes on sportfishing vacations without Margaret. As we said, he is an idiot. Is he charming? He is not. Is he handsome? Passably. What, then, is his appeal? The narrator is not sure. Anyway, one day, Stuart and Phillipe were standing near each other at one of the many birthdays, bar mitzvahs and christenings at which they find themselves. As they were talking about sportfishing, which at least means Phillipe will not talk about the ineffectivness of the UN, Phillipe noticed, at the corner of the building, a young boy being taunted by three others. Before Stuart could react, Phillipe sprinted toward the scrum, and chased away the offenders, and was soon consoling the young boy, who after a few minutes was laughing at Phillipe's jokes. When Phillipe returned to the gathering, Stuart, who saw the entire scene unfold, patted Phillipe on the back and said, 'Phillipe, you're a good man.' Stuart said this very seriously, because he was very impressed by Philippe's heroics, and because the words 'good man' are used with the utmost sincerity in his family. In fact, the primary aspiration of the men in his family is to be called, by their father or grandfather or Great-Uncle Alastair, a 'good man'. So Stuart called Phillipe a good man, and though he felt initially that he might have jumped the gun, that one decent act doesn't necessarily define a man, Stuart was surprised to see that over the next weeks and months, Phillipe seemed to change. He stood straighter, he showed up on time. He was kind to, even chivalrous to, Margaret, and began a steady job. He sent her and two of her friends to a weekend spa, and fixed the broken door to her closet. Phillipe never said a word about being called a good man, and Stuart couldn't be sure that the words had any effect on him. But the change in him was clear: he was becoming what Stuart had called him, a good man, and Stuart wondered if we, all or any of us, are so easily improved. If all we need is this kind of semantic certainty. If to be named is to be realized. If once something like that is settled – I *am* a good man! – we no longer need to struggle, to guess, to err.

The Definition of Reg

The man, named Reg, works in a small office. He is twenty-seven years old. There are three people in Reg's office: Reg; an older woman named Bea; and a man named Stu, who is about forty. They all get along well, and talk often during and after work, about a wide range of subjects. One Friday, when their boss has encouraged all of them to dress more casually if they so choose, Reg comes to work in a short-sleeved polo shirt and khaki pants. Stu, who is married and straight, comments on what Reg is wearing. 'I didn't know you were so buff!' Stu says. Reg is standing about four feet from Stu, removing a new dry-erase board from its packaging, and Stu is looking him over. 'I always thought you were kind of skinny,' Stu says, 'but you're well-built, man! Like a jock! Do you work out?' Reg shrugs and tells Stu that he doesn't work out, but sometimes plays lacrosse, a sport he played in college. Stu is still looking him over. 'Well, you should wear stuff like that more often. That shirt's good on you. Chicks would dig that, I bet. You gotta show off those pipes,' he says, now pointing to Reg's arms. Reg is hoping he is not blushing and Stu is not finished: 'You've got nice shoulders, Reg. You swim?' Reg admits that he did a bit of swimming as a young man. 'Looks like it,' Stu says. 'Man, you think you know a guy, then he comes to work like some kind of Adonis!'

There is a long pause as Reg wonders if Stu is finished commenting on his body, and while Stu continues to examine Reg, deciding if there is any more commenting that needs to be done. Finally Stu's phone rings, and he turns to answer it and the moment is over. Reg returns to his desk and tries to work. How can he work? He feels touched, massaged. He feels as if he's been slathered with peanut butter and that Stu has licked it off. Reg is straight, and knows that Stu is straight, and that he doesn't mean anything sexual by his comments, but still Reg wonders, briefly, what it would be like to kiss Stu. He imagines the bristles of Stu's goatee against his own chin. He wonders if Stu's tongue, if men's tongues generally, are thicker than women's. He tries to work, but finds he cannot concentrate. Is he in love with Stu or in love with his own body, now that it has been immortalized by Stu's gorgeous words? He cannot sit still. He goes to the bathroom and flexes his arms. He pushes his sleeves up a bit to reveal more bicep. He masturbates into the toilet. He jogs in place. He returns to his desk and writes down Stu's exact words. He daydreams of spending more time with Stu, basking in his approval, in being appreciated this way. All Reg has ever wanted, he now realizes, is this kind of thing, to be gazed at, to be admired. It electrifies every part of him; it's more pleasing to him than the affirmation of any work he's ever done or could do, and he wants more of it. He wants it always, and he finds himself wondering how far – into a different lifestyle, as a gay man, as a young man dating an older man, as a seducer, as a homewrecker – he would be willing to go to get it. He wonders how to tell Stu that if this is going to work, Stu will need to lose some weight, because right now he looks like a goddamned heifer.

How Long It Took

How long did it take? It took eight days. Ursula had been seeing Tomas for almost a year – though not so frequently because they both sold paper products, very bright paper products and thus traveled a lot – when one Tuesday, he referred to her neighbor as 'that Oriental wench'. Ursula and Tomas were unpacking groceries, and he was trying to remember the name of the neighbor (Grace), whom he did not like, and he thought it prudent to refer to her this way, as 'that Oriental wench'. In the space of a few seconds, Ursula passed through shock, through dismay, briefly resting in amusement, and settling in a feeling of total unrelenting despair. She should have known he was a moron. She should have investigated more thoroughly his brain before enjoying his body, which was taut and hairless and clean. But now they had been together for too long, and she had been, for all these many months, the paramour of a dipshit. Ursula wanted to be with future-people, people advancing tolerance and understanding and the linguistic corollaries thereof. But instead she'd been pleasuring – again and again – the unreconstructed ghost of all past prejudice, in the form of this tall chiseled man of broad shoulders and long lashes. And now what could she do? She spent days catatonic, balanced between disgust and a creeping longing for his legs and arms and smell. She could pretend he never said it, could ignore the implications, could call it anomalous. She made lists of men with whom she could replace him, including many of the characters from *The West Wing*, surely none of whom would say such a thing. On the seventh day he called. He apologized. He delivered to her a long note on rice paper, including a haiku of surprising delicacy. The following night, the eighth, she drank merlot alone, knowing that this man – not the man with whom she could change worlds – gave her more than any man before him, and this fact made her crazy in its perfect injustice. She called Tomas, implored him to come over, and when he arrived she rode him silly and screamed and screamed and screamed and screamed.

She Needed More Nuance

Her name was Wendy Berlin and her life was entirely too symbolic. If it were written as fiction, it would be klutzy in its clichés, its convenient ironies; no one would believe it for a second. Wendy was divorced, having been married, for seven years, to a man who finally left her (and their twin daughters, five years old) after contracting psoriasis. The seven-year itching led to his meeting with a dermatologist, Lola, who seduced him in the examination room; weeks later he was off with her and Wendy was alone. Did E. Berlin now live on the other side of the country? Of course he did. Was his new love younger than Wendy, and more attractive and more successful in most measurable ways? You know this is true. Was her name Lola? Yes, we covered this just a few moments ago. Now Wendy lived with her two daughters, who of course resembled their departed father much more than they did Wendy, giving her reason to think of her ex-husband every time she gazed upon them (which she tried not to do; she kept the house dimly lit). Their names were no help either: Faith and Joy. Their behaviors after the divorce? Faith got lost, while Joy became depressed. Soon after, they did the same thing, but in reverse. Were there other obvious and overly clear reminders of the broken marriage of these Berlins? Let's see. Years earlier, when Wendy and

Earl – for that was her husband's name – were first married, they bought a house, a ramshackle structure they began to refurbish with the optimism of newly-weds newly nesting. But when they suddenly split, the house was left unfinished; the areas in progress were bare, covered in plastic and plaster and designs written with chalk. Thus, since Earl's departure, Wendy and Faith and Joy walked through it somberly, seeing the clear evidence of a family failed, a family interrupted while – fairly literally – under construction. Wendy hadn't the money to finish it, and couldn't move for the same reason, leaving her stuck in her former life, incomplete. To fill the rooms, did one of her daughters invent an invisible friend? She did. His name? His name was 'Daddy'. Did the other daughter begin to act out in school, picking fights and biting her teachers? Of course she did. What was the season? It was late fall. Was it unseasonably cold? It was. The sky was grey, the rain came steadily, and all of this turned downward around Wendy's fortieth birthday, which landed on Christmas Eve, while her daughters were in Hawaii with Earl and Lola. Also: was it her parents' anniversary? It was their fiftieth; they were spending it in Cuba – where Earl proposed. Every other year, the fact that she'd been born on their special day had been a great joy for all involved. Now it was a cruel and none-too-subtle reminder that Wendy had failed where they had succeeded. 'Gah!' said Wendy one day, alone in her half-finished home, realizing that she could tolerate all of the aforementioned situations, she really could, if not for their plodding obviousness. She was an avid and discerning reader, and fancied herself something of a critic. Thus, all of this, every clunky metaphor and heavy-handed coincidence, grated against the very fabric of her being. Now she lived in the most hackneyed kind of literary life, and every day it became worse. Did the family dog die? He did – under the wheels of Earl's new sportscar, when he came to pick up his favorite record: an original 45" pressing of Al Green's 'Let's Stay Together'. The bitch's name? Amore.

The Heat and Eduardo

Part I

The man's name was Eduardo and he lived alone in Maine. He enjoyed the rugged seasons, did not mind the snow, the wind, the harshness of a walk to the mailbox. Inside his home, in the winters and falls, he usually wore socks, pants, a shirt and a sweater, and kept the thermostat at 62. But one night, his clothes were wet and he took them off. He had been chopping wood, had raised his ax over his head and triggered an overhead branch to dump six or so pounds of snow onto him, down his back, into his pants. So at home, in his living room, he removed the clothes and hung them to dry. Soon he was naked and cold, and knowing it would take him some time to become warm again, he turned rightward the heat-setting, to 76 degrees. The house quickly warmed, and while he was still looking for new clothes, he realized he was already warm, while still unclothed, sitting in his living room. On a lark, he continued to sit on the couch, to read a book, still naked, and he found himself enjoying the experience mightily. He wondered why he'd never done it before; it was both completely natural and utterly decadent, and he decided that from then on, he would do this every night, read naked on his sofa. But because the house had to be very warm while he read naked, he thought, it would certainly increase his heating bill significantly. Eduardo was not a rich man, thus calculations were necessary that first night. After finishing one chapter of his book, he walked over to his desk, and nakedly calculated how much more heat each day he would need to bring the home to the required 76 degrees for the two hours he guessed he needed each night. By his math, he figured it would cost about five extra dollars in gas to bring the home to the correct temperature, sending his monthly heating bill to $150 more than normal. Eduardo was saddened by this, for he knew he could not afford such an increase. He paced and frowned and pondered. Then he had an idea.

Of Gretchen and de Gaulle

There was a man, sitting in the Charles de Gaulle
Airport, who knew he was supposed to be writing the
second part of a story about someone named Eduardo,
who lived in Maine and who wanted to read naked on
his couch but needed to figure out the financing. But
this story could not be finished, because there were two
very large distractions. The first was the realization that
this Parisian airport, or at least the portion in which he
was currently in the midst of spending six hours, was
so dilapidated, so ancient and poorly designed, that he
found himself continually amazed and exasperated and
longing for Heathrow. There were no services in this
Parisian airport. There were no seats. No phones. And,
inexplicably, the restaurant referred to its French fries
as 'American Potatoes'. It was beyond hope. The second
and more distracting distraction for this airport-writing-
man was his knowing that another, more pressing story
had yet to be told. This more crucial story concerned
an enormous squid named Gretchen, who was living in
the Caspian Sea and who wanted more than anything
to be an accountant. Gretchen's family had always been
supportive of her hobbies and interests, but she knew
her parents would never approve of her wanting to
become an accountant for a major international
accounting or consulting firm. They would never under-

stand her longing to wear a smartly tailored suit, black pumps and glasses, to prepare the yearly returns for a Fortune 500 company, to find tax loopholes in unexplored places. This is what she wanted, more than anything – the suit, the office, the papers and PCs, the drinks afterward at a downtown TGI Friday's – but she didn't know where to start. Surely most of the best accounting schools, for example the University of Illinois, were not accustomed to admitting giant squids into their programs. And even if her parents consented, even if the school did admit her, as some sort of diversity-building experiment, there would no doubt be discrimination, misunderstandings. The other students would wonder, for example, if Gretchen would at any moment grab one of them with her powerful suckers and then quickly grind them up with her razor-like beak and then devour their eviscerated remains. And could she guarantee that she wouldn't? Sadly, she could not. She was very good with numbers, yes, but she was also a giant carniverous squid, and one with a ravenous appetite. Nevertheless, we invite you to write letters of support for Gretchen's accounting school admission. Address correspondence to the University of Illinois, School of Accounting, 34 Green Street, Urbana, IL, 61820, USA. Thank you.

The Heat and Eduardo

Part II

His idea was this: What if he wore *socks*? Aha! His feet were the most easily chilled part of his body, thus if he took care of them with good wool socks, certainly the rest of his body could be warm at, say, 73 degrees. That brought the daily increase down to $4, the monthly to $120. But this still was much too high. How much, he wondered, could he really afford to spend on two hours of naked reading? He paced and frowned, lied to himself – $100 – and then was truthful: $80. He could afford $80 for two hours of naked nightly reading. How would he get the $80? He could ask his mother, who was in her late seventies and lived in Cleveland, but she would, possibly, think his request frivolous. So for the $80 he would have to work. He could do an extra shift at his job – he made kielbasas – two days a week to scrounge the $80. Another few thousand kielbasas and he'd have the $80, fine. But for $80, the highest he could set the thermostat would be 67 degrees, which would be, come to think of it, a bit chilly for his shoulders, which, next to his feet, were most sensitive to the cold. Okay then: a shawl of some kind. He could wear the wool socks on his feet and a shawl of some kind on his shoulders, leaving the rest of him naked and content at 67 degrees. So the next night, he tested the 67 degrees and found it chilly not just for his shoulders and feet, but for the tops of his thighs. The tops of his thighs were less than comfortable, and when they were less than comfortable, naked reading was not pleasurable. So he added his cat, a mangy and mercurial thing named Condoleeza, to the plan. Condi would sit on his thighs, warming them. The socks would cover his feet, and the shawl his shoulders. It was perfect, yes. But no. Condi would not comply. Condi wanted to sit on his head. Eduardo's head, however, was not cold. Eduardo made his case to Condi, who was intractable. She made a gap-toothed sort of feline smirk and began to walk away. Thankfully, Eduardo had Velcro. He grabbed the cat and he affixed a wide strip of Velcro to each of his thighs, and found that Condi's coarse fur – she did not bathe – held to it tenaciously. And thusly he settled in: thermostat at 67, socks on feet, shawl on shoulders, Condi fastened to his thighs. She was not happy, Eduardo was in heaven.

Sleep to Dreamier Sleep Be Wed

Part I

There was a group of people, called the Americans, who once had a very vivid nightmare, simultaneously. The nightmare, which lasted many years, was nightmarish in many ways – but one notable facet was that in this nightmare the vice-president of their country was someone so outwardly and cartoonishly evil that his existence seemed ludicrous and wholly unbelievable, even in a nightmare. In the history of nightmare-villains and movie-villains and villains drawn with crayons by troubled children, this man stood above them all, though he was not very tall. Or maybe he was tall, but it was impossible to tell, given he walked very much like a hunchback, his head set deep into his shoulders and favoring one side. This way of walking seemed suspect, but it was nothing compared to the way he spoke. He spoke out of a small and dark corner of his mouth, in a way that was so comically fiendish that it seemed a put-on. If an improvising actor, asked to conjure a bad man or perhaps a minion of Satan, conceived of such a way of talking, his acting coach would say 'No, no. Pull back. Way back. We're doing the vice-president here – not Marty Feldman in *Young Frankenstein*.' But this was indeed the way the vice-president spoke and walked. And his laugh? A mirthless thing, a chilling 'Heh heh heh' – again, emitted from a dark corner of his mouth – accompanied by a forced shaking of his round fleshy back. Yes, yes – a fleshy back that was, like the rest of him, always sweating. Or it seemed always to be sweating, every inch of him, oozing with oil and perspiration and, perhaps, small brown-black worms that would leave and enter him via his pores, their bidding known only to him. Was he impervious to death? He seemed to be. Over the years of this nightmare-life, God had tried, four or five times, to kill this man, by striking his heart. But each time the man's heart was struck, the vice-president laughed his rat-rat-tat laugh and shook his fleshy back, mocking God in much the same way that vampires mock certain crosses, or, say, anal leakage mocks olestra.

Part II

The people called Americans could not, it seemed, wake up from this nightmare wherein their two highest-ranking elected leaders were so clearly the wrong people for their positions, so ill-meaning in every way, that the situation defied even Nixonian standards of White-House-based nefariousness. The most fiendish player in this nightmare, as we were explaining in the last installment, was the vice-president, whose name cannot be uttered here for fear of upsetting children and plants and clouds. Suffice it to say that he was more evil than the designers of Happy Meals or the makers of smokeless tobacco, and the Americans dreamt dreams of him, constantly and without end. The Americans as a group were asleep for many years and were experiencing wretched dreams full of exploding children and men beheaded on TV, of ever-present fire and screaming and eyes everywhere wanting murder. The Americans were trapped in, it was thought, one collective red-black dream, and the only way that they could awaken from the dream was for most of the dreaming Americans to choose to wake up. But the problem was – the very strange problem – was that half of those dreaming chose to remain in this dream. (Did we say dream? Have we been saying dream? It was a nightmare, of course. A nightmare unlike any other, a nightmare that felt like the wearing of a lead cloak without holes for air or sight.) So while about half of those sleeping wanted to awaken, the other half watched, indeed, lived in, this very upsetting dream full of flames and blood and they said, 'I think this dream is okay,' or 'This is the best dream to be dreaming right now,' or even 'It would only get worse if I chose to awaken.' This was, of course, very frustrating to those who wished to wake up. Those who wished to awaken stirred and turned restlessly. They grabbed the covers, they opened windows, they moaned and coughed and kicked. But nothing, it seemed, would work. The sleepers slept and slept and even, sometimes, nodded and smiled when they watched and listened to the two men leading their nightmare. The two men would say to them, 'Have you enjoyed the nightmare thus far? Because if you love the aforementioned exploding children and endless fire, we have more – so very much more! – of that, to come.'

Part III

The people called Americans continued to sleep. As we mentioned earlier, they existed in a collective nightmare, which was shaped and guided by their highest-ranking leaders, including the most creepy and – overtly, comically – evil-like person to hold high office since . . . well, the comparison is difficult. Who would compare, in a democracy at least? Would Thatcher rank this high? (Discuss.) Anyhoo, this particular wretched person was named Cheney (Dick), and though everyone knew he was a bad man, there was a large group of the sleeping Americans who chose, apparently, to think of him as cute-bad, as opposed to truly bad-bad. That is, they knew that while in Congress he had voted against the honoring of Martin Luther King, Jr and Nelson Mandela, and for logging the living shit out of every forest known to man, and against pre-school for disadvantaged children, and against about a thousand other things that seemed reasonable enough to reasonable people. But still they thought, well, yes, he is quite creepy and very evil-seeming in every conceivable way . . . but isn't he, somehow, so evil-seeming that he's actually kind of cute? Sort of like David Bowie in *Labyrinth* or Dennis Hopper in *Blue Velvet*? You know that kind of evil that's so ridiculous that you almost like the evildoer, because they're so willing to go out and camp it up? This is what the sleepers of America thought about Dick Cheney, who kept them living in a constant nightmare from which they could not awaken. He and his little friend, who looked like a turtle, told the Americans that the nightmare was a dream, that chaos was safety, that blood was gold, that their feet were actually their mouths, that leprechauns were hippos and that cookies were shrubbery. And so many sleeping Americans thought it all so ludicrous that they kept sleeping, because waking up would surely deprive them of such rich entertainment. Meanwhile, though, the other half of the American sleepers, those who wanted to awaken from the nightmare-dream, were trying like mad to awaken the sleepers, and thus awaken the collective body of Americans. All had to awaken at once! And this was very hard, for everyone was very tired. What would it take, the wanting-to-awakens thought. How to rise from this state of near-coma? They kicked and screamed to no avail. They rang bells and threw cold water on the bed. But in the end, do you know what did it? What woke up the willing sleepers and allowed the nation to rise from this red-black slumber? Neither do I. This story needs a good ending. Please send help.

On Seeing Bob Balaban in Person Twice in One Week

Bob Balaban is a character actor who usually plays similar characters. Or they seem similar, because Bob Balaban looks so distinct. Because he is diminutive, bald, projecting an intelligence and nervous energy in league with Woody Allen and Wallace Shawn, he cannot play someone tall, or someone athletic, or someone Teutonic or dim-witted. Bob Balaban has been in the movies made by Christopher Guest, and he has been in other movies, too, including *Gosford Park*, which took place in some other time and place and starred many British actors and was sad. The point is that one week, in New York City, we saw Bob Balaban twice, in person. The first time we saw Bob Balaban he was on the street, on the Upper West Side, or perhaps Midtown, or perhaps somewhere between the two. He was walking next to a construction site, and looked very much like Bob Balaban. He was no taller or shorter than we would have expected – not heavier or lighter, not balder or more fully haired. We said nothing to him and no one else seemed to take notice of his presence. The second time we saw him was three days later. He was at a party, a large one, in a nightclub in Times Square, and he was leaving. Again he looked like Bob Balaban. We have rarely seen actors out and about, and saw perhaps three actors all the time we lived in New York, which gave the dual-Balaban sightings an unsettling aftertaste. What did it mean that Bob Balaban seemed to be circling us, triangulating us? Though he seemed to be a decent man, and a very good actor, he does exude an air that could be considered nefarious, or plotting, or perhaps evil. We are not saying that he is evil, or that he is a deputy of the devil or anything of the sort. We are saying only that we cannot rule it out, because he conforms to many accepted visualizations of Satan's minions-in-human-form, and because he appears to follow around simple people like us, as we travel around New York with a pureness of heart that certainly is annoying to one such as he, who very well might have on his mind the over-throw of the city and/or the enslaving of mankind. But again, we're not saying that he is evil incarnate, we're only saying that it's a possibility, and that the people of Great Britain should not travel to New York until all of this is figured out. Also: don't go to Akron, Ohio, because we once saw Joe Pantoliano there, at an ATM, and though we loved his work on *The Sopranos*, he looked very much like he wanted to gargle human blood.

When He Started Saying
'I Appreciate It' After 'Thank You'

He was fifty years old when he began to do this, to say 'I appreciate it' each time he said 'Thank you.' He said these words during interactions with clerks, bus drivers, cabbies, cashiers, bellhops, telephone operators. While for the first four or so decades of his life it seemed enough to say 'Thank you' or 'Thanks' or 'Thanks a lot,' now he seems invariably to add 'I appreciate it,' or more accurately, ''Preciate it,' to his Thank yous. He can't pinpoint when this happened, but it's now involuntary, it's constant, and the odd thing is, the strange twist, is that he damn well means it every time. He really does appreciate it when people do kind things for him, no matter how trivial, no matter how expected they might be in their line of work. He is thankful when any human interaction goes off without a hitch, so thankful that his heart gets down on its knees in gratitude, and his mouth translates this into words: ''Preciate it.' Has he had so many ugly interactions in his life that he feels thankful for those that go smoothly? Perhaps. At his age, they have added up – the tussles with congenitally angry people, the random misunderstandings, the clashes with the uncompromising or crazy. All he wants now is to pass through days without rancor. Days without rancor. He should engrave that on his door, tattoo it on his chest. Does he fear people? He does not. Is he affected when his meeting of a new person, in any context, goes poorly? He is devastated. For days he carries with him the sneers of surly pharmacy counter-persons, the inexplicable rage of the woman whose long-leashed dog got caught up in his legs and who somehow blamed *him*, the entangled! These conflicts affect him too much, he knows. Every one brings him close to a precipice from which he seems destined to fall into a two-day funk, and thus when instead of being pushed over he is pulled back and embraced, even the slightest amount – is extended the most basic human courtesy – he finds himself soaring. Seeing his life as a series of potential skirmishes, he appreciates, damned well 'preciates, peace of any kind.

You'll Have to Save That for Another Time

You are at dinner and you want to tell your wife about how you beat your brother, who is four inches taller than you, at basketball. You have just remembered to tell her this. You beat him earlier in the day, it was so sunny and windless, and you forgot to tell her sooner but now you will tell her, as soon as she is done telling her story about the pregnant friend who slept with her ex-husband on a boat, with her current husband on the boat, too. When she is done with this story and you have commented on the story, because it is a good story, you will tell her about beating your brother at basketball. You haven't beaten him in years – since his height shot past yours when he was sixteen, and he became more skilled at basketball and just about every sport – and you feel that having beaten him will improve your virility in her eyes. Finally, her story is winding down. There is some mention of the police being called in to intercede between the friend and husband and ex-husband, on the dock, in what became a very vocal and potentially violent squabble, and your wife is laughing her full-throated laugh about it all. You are getting ready to tell your own news from the day, which in its small way means that you are not irreversibly getting older and slower and less capable of notable physical achievements, that perhaps the course you are on is not one of steady decline, but of dips and spikes, a descent less dramatic and laughable. And just as she is finishing her story and you are about to begin your own, as your mouth is actually open, forming the first words of your account, you realize that you didn't, in fact, beat your brother at basketball today. You were ahead for a while, and then eventually lost. But it was while you were ahead that you thought about how great it would be to tell your wife about beating him.

Woman, Foghorn

The woman was beloved in her town, a landlocked hamlet where she'd lived for many years. Everyone knew her name there, everyone waved when she walked by or peddled by on the tandem bicycle she rode alone, wearing a fedora once owned, she insisted, by Peter Lorre. All was good for her in this community, and the community considered her essential. One day, though, she decided it was time to move to a town with a foghorn. She had been born, many decades earlier, in a seaside village where ships would be warned when the fog was thick and the surf unruly. She heard this sound – a gentle warning, like the wail of a whale or the bleat of an elephant – while in school, while in bed, while eating ribs outside on the deck, with her father, who'd been a longshoreman. And now, thirty-five years removed from the village of her birth, she missed the sound, or believed that she missed the sound, and believed that moving back to a place featuring fog and horns and water and ships would shake her from the slump, the funk, the valley – whatever it was in which she currently found herself. The rest of this story is about the Bush administration. Have you heard, friends in England, that John Ashcroft, our attorney general, has authorized the FBI to visit the homes of those planning to protest the upcoming Republican convention?

This is true. The FBI has arrived on the doorsteps of college students, of middle-aged hippies, of people with no criminal records whatsoever who Ashcroft has deemed potentially dangerous to the security of the nation. In the United States this has made the news, but in a very quiet way, buried in the back pages of our periodicals. But good lord! This is truly, absolutely the last straw, wouldn't you say? This is the stuff of totalitarianism – the intimidation of dissenters? Bejeesus and holy fuck! If your own monkey boy, Tony B, doesn't stand up against this sort of thing – it being a clear violation of the human rights understood by our arm-locked nations – doesn't that make him complicit? I guess it's far too late for him to care. The saddest thing about this, and also the most pragmatically advantageous, is that this is the sort of outrageousness that very well might turn a few of our 4 percent undecided – many of whom lean toward libertarianism and hate this kind of shit – finally against G. W. Not that Iraq moved them, nor Guantanamo, nor Abu Ghraib, nor the gutting of the environment and rollback of all science and the spirit of progress and light and intellectual curiosity. While none of those things might have moved the dwindling undecideds, maybe this will, and though it's a terrifying price to pay, it will, in the end, be worthwhile. As for the woman of the foghorns, she actually got hit by a bus before she could move away. It was so sad.

How do the Koreans Feel
About the Germans?

You are sitting in a movie theater, waiting for the previews to start, exploring a scratchiness at the back of your throat which makes you feel both feline and distressed. You are plumbing your throat as best you can with the heel of your tongue, and while doing so, you are wondering how the Germans feel about the Koreans, and vice versa. You know generally how Americans feel about Germans (it's complicated) and how Americans feel about Koreans (we don't have such pronounced views) but you don't have any idea how the Germans feel about the Koreans, and how the Koreans feel about the Germans. You first surmise that they probably don't think too much of each other either way. Then you remind yourself that everyone has opinions about Germany, so you deduce that the Koreans probably have more distinct ideas about the Germans than the other way around. But do the Germans think much about the Koreans? You want to ask a German, but you don't really know any Germans. Not well enough to call on the phone, for sure. In college there was Sabine, who was from Frankfurt, in the US on a tennis scholarship. She was beautiful and broad-shouldered, and didn't, even distantly, think of you in a romantic way. After a few weeks of friendship, in the way you have assumed thereafter is common to all Germans, she told you of her complete disinterest, in clear and unvarnished language. But beyond Sabine, do you have any Germans you could ask about the Koreans? Perhaps you could call an embassy. But it's after 9 p.m., and you need to know now. You need to know now how the Germans feel about the Koreans before the previews start. You turn to the older couple behind you, he with a beard and she with a small goiter, and you ask them about this, about how the Germans feel about the Koreans. The man says, 'That's an odd question,' and goes back to eating a sandwich he has brought with him. The woman, however, gives the question some thought and says, 'I would imagine the Germans would feel the same way we all feel about all of the so-called foreign peoples of the world: we wish them freedom and safety and hope. And besides, are we all that different? Aren't we all getting more alike? Aren't the people of the world heading toward some kind of giant amalgam, a human Pangea, if you will? Wouldn't that be interesting – the continents drift apart, the universe expands, but at the same time, people become ever-more the same, all whirled together by th—' And at that point you lose track of what the goiter-woman is saying, because the previews have begun. Man, that Garry Marshall seems to have done it again!

Georgia Is Lost

Rodney is looking for his daughter. He's looking desperately for his daughter, Georgia, who is tiny, only two, and has run off from the bowling alley and is presumed lost. Today is her Uncle Baz's birthday party; he insisted on a bowling theme because he must always be offbeat and clever. Georgia loves her Uncle Baz (Rodney's brother-in-law) but somewhere between the second and third frames, she disappeared and now everyone is looking for her. Rodney's wife, Pollyanna, is losing her mind. People are desperate. Someone has called the police. The partygoer-bowlers are running around the alley, the parking lot, the streets surrounding; all are calling Georgia's name. Pollyanna, after joining the search for ten minutes, has now collapsed into a puddle by the vending machines, weeping. 'Someone took my daughter!' she moans. Rodney has searched the bar, the snack area and the bathrooms. He has sent two of the party's attendees to their cars, to comb the neighborhood, and while Rodney is looking for Georgia, he can't help hoping – he is so, so ashamed the thought has entered his mind – that Baz doesn't find her first. It would be just like Baz. Baz the Baztard. Baz the pisswad who has, since Georgia was born, made sure that everyone – especially Georgia – thinks he, and not Rodney, is the girl's primary male presence or focus or role model, or whatever the hell the term is. His Christmas gifts have to be bigger, more obscene. His weekend outings have to be more spectacular and unforgettable and well-thought-out. Archery! Whale-watching! Glass-blowing! Baz is a putz. He makes his own clothes, wears clogs at home, and insisted last year on defacing poor Georgia's room with a floor-to-ceiling mural of the signing of the Magna Carta. 'Uncle Baz!' Georgia could say that before she could say 'Daddy' or 'Food' or even 'No.' And now Baz is running around, his fanny-pack bouncing off his bloated ass, calling out Georgia's name. Rodney is running, too, thinking Please God, let it be me, let it be anyone but Baz – let anyone but Baz find my daughter. And his hair! Did he really wear barrettes that one day at the beach? Does he really color his greying hair with brown shampoo? Why can't Georgia see through that kind of narcissism? Oh Georgia, where are you? And why doesn't he have a real job? He's a 'life coach'? What the fuck kind of gig is that? If he had a real job he wouldn't be around every goddamned day when Rodney got home from work. He wouldn't be chasing Georgia through the house, both of them shrieking like pigs, Georgia passing her own father like he was a hat-rack, wanting only more of Uncle Baz, Uncle Baz! Uncle Baz with the ankle tattoo, the legs of a satyr and the ass of an ass. Well, for once Rodney will not come second when it comes to his own daughter. Not this time. No chance. For once – Oh no. Oh lord. Please no. Here he comes. Yes, I see who you found, Baz. Hello honey. Thanks Baz. Yes, I was scared, too. Yep, she's lucky to have her Uncle Baz. Aren't you, Georgia? I just don't know how to repay you, Baz. I guess I'll have to start thinking about that. I'm gonna get started right away, about just how best to repay you, our good Uncle Baz.

They Decide To Have No More Death

There is a group of friends, fifteen of them in all, who have known each other a very long time. In one year, three of them have died, leaving twelve. They are too young, this group of friends, to have had three of their ranks taken. So one day in May, in a house on a ridge overlooking a valley of heather and wheat, they meet to discuss what to do. After seven hours of ideas and deliberation, they decide that there will be no more death. They agree that none of them will themselves die, and that they will as a group work together to find a cure for this problem of dying too young. One of the group, Helen, draws up a petition and they all sign it. Another, Suze, begins, with twine and clay, to work on an anti-death device. Four more – Wilt, Bob, Antaea and Roy – build a lab in the basement, where they begin to experiment with gene therapy and thunder. At night they all sit on the floor by the fire and recount what they've accomplished, and speak about their friends who are gone. They talk about how Morgan, twenty-seven, heart condition, thought he could sing, though he could not sing, and how perfect he would have been for that recent TV show wherein the worst would-be crooner wins $100,000. Ginger was twenty-six and was killed when a train derailed instead of carrying her home. All of those assembled on the warm floor compare stories of when they first found out that Ginger's sweet, ebullient façade belied a quick cutting wit and X-ray eyes. One or two of them finds comfort in knowing that because these people – Morgan, Ginger, Richard – are gone and will do no more living, their lives can be summed up and dissected and turned into comprehensible narratives. A few of the assembled do this, silently, and smile at their concoctions. The fire continues in the house and moths jump from the lamps to the windows to the ceiling and back again. Everyone talks and laughs but no one tells themselves stories about Richard, because Richard took his life, flew from a bridge, and no one wants to think about this because it might mean – almost assuredly did mean, they felt – that it was, in part, their fault. Who looked away? Whose door was not open? They go to bed, content in knowing that they have spent a good day doing good work (trying to solve this problem of dying too soon) and have done a good job of not talking about Richard. The next day they awake, none having slept but pretending they have, and they go back to work. Timothy and Tanya build a catapult that would send a person to safety if death was approaching. Chrissy and Giacomo discover a way to live, forever, in mirrors made using smoke. And Mary – she with the mouth of a hundred curves – suggests that the remaining members procreate as much as possible, and overwhelm death with sheer numbers. Death will retreat, she says. Death will move on, knowing it cannot kill us all. And because Mary is the smartest of the group, and because her idea seems so practical and within reach, they all put aside what they're working on and work on her plan, first.

Roderick Hopes

Roderick is in his kitchen, hoping. He is pouring grape-
fruit juice into his souvenir Enron coffee mug, hoping
with great psychic effort. He knows that his wife, Janice,
will awaken soon, and will spend a few minutes in the
bathroom, and after her few minutes in the bathroom,
she will walk toward the kitchen and to him, and at that
time she is very likely to talk about how much sleep she
did not get. Roderick is hoping, hoping with such effort
that his knees are making noise, that she will not do
this today. Roderick and Janice have been married only
a few months, and did not live together before their
marriage, and thus he was not aware, pre-nuptials, of
this habit of hers, of informing him every day of how
little she has slept. There are slight variations to how
she delivers this information – 'I didn't sleep a bit last
night'; 'I laid awake with my head vibrating'; 'I didn't
fall asleep till four, and I've been up since five!' – but
deliver it she does, each morning over breakfast, thinking firstly that Roderick is interested in this information
and, secondly, that Roderick will believe her news, even
though Roderick knows quite well that she sleeps just
as much as he does, which is an average and adequate
amount. So Roderick butters his bagel and hopes. He
adds some jam to his bagel and wishes. Then he hears
the creak of the mattress, the turn of the doorknob,

and sees her entry into the bathroom. It will not be long now, he knows, until she will come to tell him the groggy news. 'Oh *lord*, I'm so *tired*,' she will say, and he will tense up like a prisoner flogged. How can he tell her, politely, that he doesn't goddamned for one second give a rip about her sleep or motherboning lack thereof? Is he supposed to feel *complicit* with the forces who steal sleep? Is he expected to *do* something about finding or creating more sleep for her? He refuses to forever feel guilty about sleeping soundly while she does not – but she does! – and thus he decides that if she really wants to get knocked out, he can and will accommodate her. There are sleep-aid drugs – Tylenol PM, Ambien, codeine, morphine – that he could slip into her late-evening hot chocolate (for she refuses to take anything drug-like, even aspirin). He wonders, as he cuts and carves his cantaloupe, about perhaps-more-permanent solutions to her problem, and then catches himself. Might her daily complaints about missed rest drive him to send her off to a more . . . indefinite kind of slumber? Would it all, could it all, possibly be that tidy? His eyes widen, and a grin involuntarily overtakes his face. What would be the formula – twenty Ambien, thirty or more? – and, if successful, and even if caught, would any jury convict him? He brings the cold spoon to his mouth and sucks on the orange melon flesh. He looks up in time to see her padding slowly toward him. 'Look who's all happy and well-rested,' she says so sourly the walls bend inward. 'Will I ever know the peace you know?' She frowns theatrically. He nods. 'Soon, my love, you will.'

POCKET PENGUINS

POCKET PENGUINS